My Brother's Keeper

Michael Banister

Ravenous Press, 2013

Every now and then I'm reminded of how a chain of events can unfold from something seemingly inconsequential. My nephew Josh's phone call from Manhattan last year is a good example. He was taking a lunch break at his hair salon in Soho and wanted to run an idea by me. Josh was 33 years old, the only son of my deceased younger brother Winston and Winston's former girlfriend Alexis. Winston became deceased back in 1981 when Josh was not quite three years old. Alexis was not present; they had already become a non-item by then. Winston died in the company of his new girlfriend, Julia, who died with him. You could say Winston might not have been killed had he not listened to Julia's poor advice, but then again it was only a matter of time before someone killed Winston.

Josh was born in October 1978, soon after his mom and my brother had broken up. Knowing my brother, I doubt he had ever considered Alexis to be his "one and only" girlfriend. Winston was a bit of a playboy. I well remember those days right after Josh's birth. I had just finished a six-year prison term for selling an ounce of cocaine to a narc. My wife divorced me in the middle of my prison gig. I was living, temporarily I hoped, once again at my mom's house—a 31-year-old ex-con living with his mother, his brother's ex-girlfriend, and her brand-new baby, Josh. Alexis's parents had kicked her out when they found out she was pregnant; she moved in with my mom.

Dolores, my mom, wanted another crack at raising a baby. Maybe she hoped this time she'd get a child who didn't screw up quite as badly as had two of her three children, my sister Katie being the exceptional child. Alexis was only too happy to accommodate my mom; and what choice did Alexis have, anyway?

I was disgusted with my brother for his refusal to act like a father to Josh—I remember being floored at his reply when my mom asked if he minded her helping Alexis raise the baby, "Do whatever you want, mom, but leave me out of it. I'm not gonna play father. It's not my thing. And remember, I grew up basically without a dad, and I turned out all right. This kid will do fine with two moms and a doting Uncle Mark."

4

It saddened me to hear Winston proclaim that fatherhood was not his "thing," while at the same time asserting that he had "turned out all right." Nothing could be further from the truth. I, of course, was in no position to lecture my brother, seeing as how I was a convicted coke dealer. But I did feel hurt at Win's remark that he grew up without a dad. Although our dad left the family in 1958 when Win was two, I was a pretty damn good surrogate dad. But more on that story in a minute.

My mom and Alexis rolled up their sleeves and became co-moms—first time for Alexis, fourth time for my mom, unless you also count my sister's three kids and my two kids, all of whom spent lots of time at their grandma's house when their parents were busy, sick or incarcerated.

I didn't stay around to help the co-moms raise Josh. I had to learn how to be a dad again to my own boys, ages nine and seven, after my six-year absence. Pretty soon I got a job delivering flowers for my friend Doug's business in West Oakland (I later became his business partner and ultimately the sole owner of the business). After I got my own place, I began bringing my boys over to mom's house so we could get to know Josh.

I guess it was about a year later when I began to notice the change in Winston. He popped by mom's house one Sunday and said he wanted to "do some laundry and pay a little visit to Josh." I was there babysitting a whole bunch of kids—my sister, mom and Alexis were out food shopping. Winston and I had a pretty good visit until I had to go and spoil it by asking the wrong sort of questions. "Hey, Win, what's going on with you—looks like your nostrils are getting eaten away. You using coke?"

"What if do a little blow now and then? No biggie."

"Don't give me that BS, little bro. There's a lot wrong with it. Your nose is just the first to start melting away. Your mind will go next."

"Look, Mark. I don't want any lectures from you—the ex-con and former supplier to half the coke heads in Concord."

"Okay, don't listen to me, I'm just warning you. Maybe you'll be one of the lucky ones."

"Like I said, it's no biggie. I'm not dealing. Just a little taste now and then."

I wanted to believe him but I couldn't. First of all, you don't get a coke nose job from "a little taste now and then." Second of all, he couldn't possibly afford cocaine on his pitiful part-time wages working for the Park Service in Yosemite. Remember, this was about 1979 and the $20 rock of crack cocaine was not invented yet. Powder coke was king and only royalty could afford it without selling it to pay for their habit. Winston had to be dealing. I figured that was his real reason for his "visit" to the Bay Area. Winston freely admitted he had been selling weed since 1975, when he and a bunch of his fellow "valley rats" who worked shit jobs in Yosemite heard about the dope plane that crashed in one of those little ice-covered lakes in the high country. The rumor, which turned out to be accurate, was that there were maybe a dozen huge

8

bales of weed poking up out of the ice, free for the taking by skilled winter hikers.

Win and others made several hikes up to the crashed plane that winter and brought down at least 200 pounds of weed apiece before the Park rangers found out and cleared the crash site. That was the beginning of Win's career as a dope dealer.

He bragged about those high-country trips and the "airplane weed" he "rescued." I heard all about it when he visited me in San Quentin State Prison in 1977. When he started talking about it I didn't believe him, so I didn't think to tell him to shut up talking about drugs in the prison visiting room. But later I read about the crash and the "Airplane Weed" phenom in "High Times" magazine, the dopers' bible.

I also heard about it from my mom and her sister Mary Ann, who told me about the time they returned early to my mom's house from an aborted weekend gambling trip to Reno. Just before the sisters left for Reno, Winston showed up, ostensibly to "do some laundry." Mary Ann got a kick out of telling me what happened when they returned a few hours later, before Winston had returned from doing his "errands."

"Mark, you should have seen Dolores's face when she opened the front door and saw Winston's marijuana spread out all over the coffee table, couches and kitchen counter." My mom and aunt immediately knew Winston was drying the weed.

Mary Ann related with her typical animation what they did next. "Winston wasn't home, so we immediately turned around and went to a coffee shop. We had a leisurely dinner and dawdled for an hour or so, to make sure he had returned from his errands, before calling the house. Dolores told Winston we had to cancel our Reno trip because the highway was closed due to ice and snow. After your mom told Winston that, we dawdled a little more at the shopping center before driving back to the house. When we got there all the marijuana was gone. The house did smell a little funny, though. 'The house smells sort of like a skunk,' your mom told Winston. I about died at the look on poor Winston's face when Dolores said that. Of course, your mom and me had long known he was selling marijuana, but Winston didn't know we knew." Recalling all this later made me sad all over again, because those events directly led to his demise. And several other events came about as a result of errors on my part.

Win and I were eight and a half years apart. When I was between the ages of nine and ten, I felt he was more like a son than a brother. After my parents' divorce I had to learn how to be the world's best babysitter in a hurry. My mom was a teacher and couldn't afford to stop working to raise a new baby in addition to a nine-year-old son and a six-year-old daughter. With no dad around, and with mom struggling with depression—post-partum and post-divorce—I landed the substitute dad role. My mom held it together during the week when she was teaching by hiring our cleaning woman to come to the house and take care of baby Winston until I got home from school. Mom arranged with Katie's and my elementary school for us to leave school after lunch period, so that I could take Katie home with me and take over the babysitting job. On weekends, it was all on me pretty much; my mom basically stayed in bed all weekend for those two years. I did okay until my last year of junior high, when I started staying away from home more and more. "Let Katie take care of him for awhile," was my mantra as dating and drinking and getting high took up the lion's share of my free time.

Somehow, though, despite doing my share of partying, I managed to graduate fourth in my high school class of 365 students and got a full scholarship to UC Santa Barbara, just far enough away to not have to be a substitute dad any more. By my last year in college, it seemed to me that Winston had become almost a man by the age of 12. I wasn't too surprised, really. He grew up fairly independent. By the age of four he was roaming the neighborhood all on his own most weekends. My mom used to get exasperated phone calls from neighbors several blocks away saying that Winston was in their yards or was knocking on their doors. Of course, I got the blame for that even though it was the weekend and by all rights it was my mom's job to keep an eye on him. As a result, however, Win became quite good at taking care of himself.

In December of 1968, when I was home on winter break, I gave Win a year's subscription to Rolling Stone magazine for his 13th birthday. Looking back on that, I now suspect that gift was no gift at all. That misguided publication single handedly steered

14

Win into the world of drugs, sex and rock'n'roll. One year, I remember, Rolling Stone declared cocaine "Drug of the Year," touting its reputed "non-addictive" character and sex-enhancing properties. A few months after my misguided birthday present, Winston took up the bass guitar and started smoking weed at rock concerts at the Fillmore Auditorium in San Francisco. My mom would drop him off at the auditorium and go drink coffee at Manning's Coffee Shop on Market Street while waiting for the concert to end.

Tangentially related to my tacit invitation to Win to check out the world of drugs and the counter culture, was something that happened when he was 15 and a sophomore in high school. In those days, 1970-71, our town was 100 percent blue collar, working class, and engulfed by a wave of drug use and drug dealing. I was living in Berkeley at the time, working as a book buyer at Moe's Books on Telegraph Avenue, so I was no longer involved in my hometown scene. Years later, Win told me of an incident that sent chills down my spine and explained why Win abruptly quit high school and left town to go work in Yosemite as a valley rat. Win told me that during lunch period one day, he was walking behind the campus to an isolated group of buildings behind the school when he came upon a scene that changed his life forever. I should first point out that in those days my high school had expanded from its downtown location onto a second, temporary campus in some unused buildings in a former Army base about a mile away. The school district later decided to relocate the expanded campus elsewhere, their official reason

being to get away from those somewhat derelict Army

buildings. The real reason was probably that there

were too many isolated places on and around the

campus that were very inviting to the more criminally

minded students.

That was the situation on this particular

morning as Winston was walking to some of the less-

inhabited outlying buildings to smoke some dope

before settling into a long, boring afternoon of social

studies, English and bonehead math. When he turned

the corner he saw his childhood friend Mitch

Whittaker and three other guys Win didn't recognize.

They were standing around a kid lying face down on

the ground. The kid was twitching and moaning.

Mitch and the other three guys had their backs to Win.

One of Mitch's friends handed a gun to Mitch, who then fired a shot into the kid on the ground. Win figured he must have come on the scene after the kid had been shot at least a couple of times, because the kid was not screaming like you'd expect, just kind of groaning. Win told me he recognized the kid. He was a notorious coke dealer who often as not ripped off his customers by selling them bunk dope. Win immediately guessed that this must have been what the kid had done to Mitch. After shooting the kid, Mitch turned, gun in hand, and saw Win standing there.

Win described to me the startled look on Mitch's face, a look Win never forgot. "Mark, I was never so scared in my life. But then something weird happened. A voice inside told me that Mitch would not shoot me. And it looked like Mitch was just as scared as me. He said to me, 'Win, if I were you I'd leave this town. I can't guarantee your safety. I'm serious; go.' Mark, you know that Mitch and I go way back to kindergarten days, and you know his family as well as I do. I didn't think he'd hurt me, and I think he knew I'd never rat him out. But I took his warning seriously; the guys he was with didn't know me from Adam. Those guys could be trouble. I figure I was very lucky that Mitch was the one holding the gun at that particular moment."

As Win told me this story, we were standing on our mom's front porch around midnight. It was a year before I got busted for dealing, and I was all ears. Win was headed back 'home' to his little ski cabin in the Yosemite wilderness, and I had asked him to explain exactly why he had quit high school and was living in the wilderness like that.

"That story is why, Mark. I didn't feel safe anywhere in Contra Costa County anymore, I couldn't stay in school, and I didn't want to risk anything bad happening to mom. So I split."

For the next year, before I took up residence in San Quentin, I used to see Win now and then at the homes of mutual acquaintances in Berkeley and Oakland, where Win apparently felt safe. He told me he was a seasonal worker in the Park, cutting fire trails in the spring and summer and helping the rangers rescue skiers and hikers in the winter. As I mentioned earlier, that all changed in 1975, the "Year of the Airplane," as Win described it.

Because Winston was super gregarious and the world's primo nice guy he had lots of friends in Yosemite and the nearby towns. His first girlfriend, at least the first one I knew, was Alexis, who a few years later became Josh's mom.

I got to know Alexis a little before Josh's birth, and I liked her. I still like her. We're still good friends after all these years, mostly because she's Josh's mom and an official member of our clan. Through her, I got to know my own brother a little better, too. She had lots of stories of the scene in Yosemite and El Portal, the town next to the park where she had been living back in those days, before she got pregnant, broke up with Winston, and began her short-lived stay at her parents' home in Concord. As I said, they kicked her out when her pregnancy became evident.

21

I remember the last day of Winston's life, June 25, 1981, like it was yesterday. That's the day Winston and Julia were murdered and their respective kids orphaned. I got a phone call from Winston three days earlier, a Monday. He wanted to "celebrate" something. He was very mysterious. I agreed to meet him the following Friday in Oakland.

On Thursday afternoon my sister called me, crying, and told me Win had been shot that morning. I don't know what was wrong with me, but when I heard my sister's words, "Mark, Winston's dead," I couldn't react, at least on the inside. I suppose I said something like, "Oh no, oh my God," or some such. But I remember how zombie-like I felt. Nothing inside, zilch.

Looking back I sometimes blame it on the distractions from my complicated purchase of Doug's flower business. Doug was dying of cancer and since he was my friend and had no family, he was going to sell me the business for a pittance. I was all shook up about Doug, and nervous about all the transactional formalities, so maybe that's why I didn't have much of a reaction to Win's death. Or maybe I'm just that way, too skilled at burying unpleasant emotions.

My mom and sister, on the other hand, were devastated and showed it. My sister was extremely pregnant at the time and gave birth to her youngest son three weeks later. She named the boy Winston after the uncle he would never know. My mom had an interesting reaction. After a month or so of not being able to leave the house—it was summer vacation and she wasn't teaching—she went into private eye mode. She spent many an afternoon in Martinez at the Contra Costa County sheriff's office trying to pry information out of the deputies and brass who were part of the investigation into the killings. I pitched in as soon as my purchase of the business was finalized. I got one of Doug's drivers to continue holding down the fort while I played sleuth with my mom for a couple weeks. Doug had a crew of a dozen drivers, so my presence wasn't immediately necessary.

What we found out was astonishing. It wasn't easy. The deputies at the sheriff's office didn't feel particularly inclined to help us because they suspected my brother was a drug dealer. But one of the deputies recognized my mom from an "American Criminal Justice System" class they had both taken at

UC Berkeley earlier that year. They had to take a certain number of classes each year to move up on their respective salary scales. He liked her, felt sorry for her, so he gave us copies of a bunch of documents from the file.

I couldn't believe what those documents told me. This was about six months after the murders, and the most heart-rending document was the transcript of the interrogation of a young man who apparently lived in the apartment where Winston and Julia were killed, and knew the killers. He had been persuaded to testify against the two killers, should they ever be brought to trial, in order to avoid being prosecuted as an accessory to murder. This young man described in great gory detail how the murders went down. I almost threw up as I read the transcript, and I never read it again after that.

The young man was apparently an acquaintance of Julia's and bragged to her about knowing a big-time coke dealer. Julia must have told Winston that she "knew someone who knew someone" and talked him into selling the dude a kilo of coke for $30,000. I had trouble believing that Winston, who normally was very careful about dealing only with people he knew (unlike his careless brother, who dealt with strangers one too many times), would decide to do that. But be that as it may, the temptation to make a quick 30 grand won the day, and Winston and Julia went to their deaths.

I did some more sleuthing into who the killers were and what happened to them. They were suspected of killing other people in Nevada before killing Winston and Julia. Almost a year after reading the interrogation transcript, I learned they were recently convicted of another murder in Florida and were serving life sentences. The DA in our county decided not to waste the public's money prosecuting two convicted murderers for the murder of a drug dealer and his girlfriend.

The only other distasteful thing I had to do before saying farewell to the sheriff's office was to claim Winston's wrecked Camaro. The killers had put Winston and Julia's bodies in the Camaro and pushed it down an embankment near the Carquinez Bridge. The car was not only a total wreck, but it was full of my brother's and Julia's blood. I wanted nothing to do with it. So I sold it to a salvage yard and never set foot in that area again. To this day, I avoid taking that road when I'm heading for the bridge.

Sad as all this was to me, my sister, our kids and my mom, we tried not to show our grief around Josh. He was not quite three years old. Whenever he would ask about his dad, we would just say he was gone. After a few more months, we finally broke the news to him that his daddy "went to God." We didn't supply details, at least not true details. We made up a story about how he had been killed in a car accident. Josh was sad, and even cried a little, but after awhile he was able to put it behind him.

After that I became a better uncle to Josh. But even though at the beginning I was doing that out of a sense of duty and sympathy, soon I got to know the little guy pretty well and loved him even more. He was quite a charmer, and very talented. He and his only girl cousin, my sister's daughter Maya, were always practicing lip-syncing to pop songs that they watched on MTV or VH-1. They even worked out little dance numbers that they would perform for the rest of us. As he and Maya entered their teenage years, though, they saw less and less of each other. She lived in Walnut Creek, he in Antioch. They had different sets of friends and social groups.

Alexis and my mom were good co-moms. Josh grew up to be an intelligent and responsible young man. Eventually I told Josh the whole story of his father's and Julia's murder. He had heard bits and pieces of the story from his mom, and so he was thankful when I told him the rest.

Although Josh was now living in New York, he still kept in touch with everyone, especially his only girl cousin, Maya. His strong bond to his family was probably the reason for his phone call to me last year. He told me he wanted to track down Julia's daughter. I think he was looking for the sister he never had. Josh wanted to know what I thought and whether I could help him find Julia's daughter. I thought it was an interesting idea and I told him I'd see what I could do. This is how Josh presented his idea to me.

"Here's what I think, Uncle Mark," he said in between bites of what sounded like a sandwich. "You said a couple of months ago you had found some information about Julia when you were cleaning out grandma's house."

"That's right—her parents' and daughter's names. But not their address. What do you want with that stuff? Julia wasn't your mom; I don't think she even met you. And your dad wasn't the father of Julia's little girl."

"I know, but somehow I think it might be interesting . . . no, that's such a lame word. It might be extremely fulfilling, satisfying, uplifting, something like that, if I could get in touch with them."

"How so? Pardon my ignorance, but I see no connection between you and Julia."

"The connection is hard to explain. Julia's boyfriend was my dad, and their kids might have known one another. Julia's daughter was the same age as me when her mom and my dad were murdered together."

"So, are you suggesting some kind of pseudo family reunion? Have you considered the fact that the murders occurred over 30 years ago? Or that Julia's parents might blame your father for the death of their daughter?"

"All I know is I have this strong desire to meet my counterpart, so to speak. Nothing more than that, at least for now. I dream about her. I can't get the thought out of my mind. Just picture this: her mom and my dad were lovers. They were in the same apartment when they were murdered. And their respective kids ended up living with, and maybe raised by, their respective grandparents. I can't let this picture dissolve. I have to follow up on it."

I told Josh I'd think about it. All I knew about Julia was that she had lived in Concord, California, when she was with my brother. Her parents might live in Concord, or they might have moved, or they might have passed onto their greater reward. I'd have to start phoning or writing people named Rawlings once I found the names in the phone book or on the Web.

I did know Julia's daughter's name, Kathy. I supposed I could look for "Kathy Rawlings" and see how many there were. Her name and Julia's parents' names were on the piece of notebook paper my mom had tucked away in one of her address books. I'd asked my sister and Alexis about Kathy and Julia, but neither knew anything about them. And our mom was now recently deceased, so there was no way to find out from her. My 33-year-old nephew was looking for a young woman his own age, whereabouts unknown, who maybe had been in some sort of semi-familial relationship with his dad. I had to remind myself that Josh's motive was not, definitely not, to find a girlfriend. *He's gay; he's just looking for a sister*, I reminded myself.

I must have been the only member of our clan who didn't realize Josh was gay until he was in his twenties. My sister's kids laughed when I expressed shock at my recent discovery. "Uncle Mark, we've known that for years. Where have you been?"

Where have I been, indeed? I guess I was fooled by the fact that once Josh graduated from high school, he moved into a commune in Berkeley. He was volunteering in food kitchens, protesting things like the WTO, NAFTA, and the Iraq War, and getting arrested in places like San Francisco and Seattle. It didn't occur to me that such a militant radical could be gay. Somehow, his militancy overshadowed his more feminine side, which he began to show when he was maybe 21. I finally suspected the truth when he got his hair stylist's license and moved to the Castro District in San Francisco. Stereotypes, sure, but they were like a neon sign flashing the message, "Your nephew might be gay, Mark."

Even cosmopolitan San Francisco was not exciting enough for Josh, even though he grew up in a small working-class town at the eastern end of Contra Costa County. He jumped at the chance to move to New York a couple of years later when a friend called to offer him a room in an apartment in Brooklyn. Alexis wasn't too thrilled with that idea, since it would mean fewer opportunities to visit her wonderful son, the light of her life. Plus, Alexis had just been diagnosed with breast cancer. But she didn't say anything to Josh at that point; she wanted to let him have this new experience in the Big Apple and would wait until she found out whether her particular tumor was something that might kill her.

Josh stayed in his Brooklyn apartment for about six months before he moved to lower east side Manhattan. After another six months there, he got a really lucky break. A young woman who was one of his regular customers at his salon happened to be an heiress of a publishing magnate and owned a two-bedroom flat in Soho. She only lived there part-time, preferring to spend most of her time at the family estate in Connecticut, which she also inherited. She wanted someone to live in the flat to make sure it wasn't burglarized. So she rented a room to Josh for $600 a month, with full access to the kitchen and the little yard out back. Josh was in heaven.

It was just after Josh's move into the Soho flat that he asked me to find out more about Julia's daughter. Although I didn't get around to it right away, it wasn't too difficult to find all the people named James and/or Louise Rawlings in Contra Costa County; what was difficult was narrowing the list down—there were something like 15 Rawlingses, three of whom were named James, two Jims, five "J."s, two Louises, three "L."s, and two Loises (which I added to the list just in case my mom's shaky handwriting said Lois instead of Louise). There was nobody named Kathy or "K.". The other challenge was to write to all of the ones who had their addresses included in the phone book listings.

First I wrote to the seven Rawlingses with addresses in the phone book, rather than phoning everyone. The subject matter just didn't seem to be appropriate for a phone call—"Hi, I'm the brother of the guy responsible for your daughter's murder. Can we talk?" In my letter I carefully explained the situation, how my nephew wanted to meet the person who shared the same tragedy as he did. I was careful to mention that my nephew was gay to avoid giving the impression I was trolling for a girlfriend for him. I described who I was and expressed my continuing sorrow over the whole thing. I blamed my brother for the murders with no suggestion that Julia shared any of that blame. I included my phone number. It felt a little uncomfortable to be telling this story to people who, in all likelihood, were not the people who should be reading the story.

For a solid month I was on pins and needles. The only distraction I had, and it was a pretty big one, was my business decision to implement Doug's long-dormant idea of expanding the business to include not only deliveries of flowers, but deliveries of small packages, including prescriptions and medical supplies, from pharmacies. I even added an alternative d.b.a. name—"Tyrannosaurus Rx"—to the company's formal name.

At the end of that month, one of the J.'s phoned. Mr. and Mrs. James Rawlings of Orinda were gratified at what Mrs. Rawlings ("call me Lois") said was the "character" of my letter. "You know, Mr. Hughes, it's rare enough that we get an actual letter from anyone these days, let alone such a letter as yours. It must have caused you a good bit of pain to write it. But I, and my husband Jim, think something good can come of this."

Lois invited me to have lunch with them at their favorite Orinda deli the following Saturday. I accepted. They told me all about their granddaughter. Kathy lived in Walnut Creek. Jim told me Kathy was shocked by my request to meet her and tell her about Josh. But she agreed to have me email her and we would go from there.

After a couple of emails, I took Kathy out to lunch at the Cheesecake Factory in Walnut Creek. She was a striking woman, tall, muscular, and with some premature gray streaks in her long hair. She gave a strong impression of self-assurance and maturity. She had an amazing sense of humor with a deep laugh and broad smile. In other words, she was so similar to Josh in physical appearance, personality and demeanor that it was hard to believe she and Josh didn't share the same mother and father. Although her mother had been killed and Josh still had his, they both had benefitted from the doting love of their grandparents.

She knew the whole story of her mom's and Winston's murders by drug dealers. "But, Mr. Hughes, in your letter you didn't need to blame the whole thing on your brother; my mom was equally to blame, I'm sure. Over the years, my grandparents gradually told me more and more about her wild youth, and I figured out pretty quickly that she might have had a lot to do with the bad situation she found herself in."

Kathy was laid off recently—she was an LVN at a company that provided home health care services. She had something like four years experience driving all over Contra Costa County delivering and setting up medical equipment, delivering supplies such as prescriptions, and providing nursing care for a growing number of house-bound invalids, until those patients' illnesses necessitated a transfer into the county's hospice program.

She was more than willing to correspond with Josh. For my part, I not only gave her Josh's email and address and phone numbers, I offered her a job with my company right on the spot. I needed a few more drivers, especially ones who had Kathy's experience, and I told her I would look into having T-Rx and Kathy provide limited home nursing care as part of its medical home delivery service.

Kathy accepted, even though I was worried she would be put off by the location of the company in a very rough part of West Oakland. "Not a problem, Mark ('Mark' already!). My former company had clients all over Richmond; it doesn't get any worse than North Richmond, let me tell you."

It took me a few days to get all the paperwork in order. Then I called Josh with the good news, in particular something I found in Kathy's paperwork that would be sure to bowl him over: "Josh, not only is she a perfect fit for my company, she has the same birthday as you and even resembles you in many ways!" That was the icing on the cake in Josh's estimation—not only a new "sister" in a spiritual sense, but a kind of doppelganger as well.

I waited almost a week before calling Alexis to let her know about tracking down Kathy, feeling a little strange about telling her about the daughter of the deceased girlfriend of Alexis's ex-boyfriend. Alexis surprised me—Josh had already talked to his mom. She had no problem and thought it was a good idea.

Another month went by and Kathy was turning out to be one of the best drivers I had. Not only that, she was full of useful suggestions about streamlining the routes—I had drivers running all over Contra Costa, Alameda, San Francisco, Marin and San Mateo Counties. Kathy had a talent for organization.

A funny thing happened the following month. It turned out that one of Kathy's deliveries was to Alexis, whose recurrence of cancer required her to temporarily live with her mom, Sylvia. Her dad, who had been the one responsible for kicking Alexis out decades earlier, had long since passed away. Alexis was bedridden with nausea from one of the last infusions in her second round of chemotherapy. She needed her various meds delivered because her aging mom was essentially housebound and didn't drive. When I got the order from Alexis's pharmacy I decided to give the delivery to Kathy without telling her who it was for. I did, however, let Alexis and Sylvia in on the little joke. I would love to have been there when Alexis's mom answered the door and Kathy asked if Alexis Ramirez lived there. Kathy told me that she and Alexis had a nice chat and promised to get together when Alexis was feeling better.

Alexis's recovery from that round of chemo finally was completed around the end of July of last year and she was pronounced cancer free. She called me and Josh to tell us the worst of it was over. She said Josh told her he wanted to come out to California in October to celebrate her recovery and his birthday. He would stay with her and grandma Sylvia.

I decided to spring yet another surprise on Kathy, this time regarding Josh's October visit. Alexis and I invited my sons and the "Brady Bunch" (my sister Katie's family) to Sylvia's to celebrate Josh's and Kathy's mutual birthday, as well as to celebrate Alexis's finally being told she was cancer free. I told Josh about the party, of course, but not Kathy. I simply gave Kathy another T-Rx delivery to Alexis's mom's house, but this time ostensibly for Sylvia. The surprise was perfect. I could see that Josh and Kathy had a great time at the party. Kathy told me she and Josh had lunch a few days later, and after that she drove him to the airport for his return flight to JFK.

The final link in the chain of serendipity appeared when Josh called me in March of this year, almost a year after he phoned me with his request to help him track down Julia's daughter. He told me he was going to give up on New York. "The winters are too cold, Uncle Mark. This past one—actually it's still blowing a mean blizzard here in Manhattan—was the last straw. That, plus I lost my job at the salon."

"How did that happen?"

"You remember I told you at the birthday party my boss had promoted me to office manager at the salon? Well, eventually, he decided to sell the business to me. His motivation for wanting to sell was his diagnosis of advanced prostate cancer. But he died the end of January before we could consummate the deal. His brother, a died-in-the-wool homophobe, inherited the salon and refused to finish the deal with me. Instead, he sold the business to a chain and I was out of a job."

"Shit, that's terrible, Josh! What are you gonna do?"

"I really don't know. I guess look around in the Castro again like before. Maybe I can find something. But I really don't relish spending the rest of my life doing nothing but cutting hair again; I was getting to like the business aspects of running the salon."

At that moment, I had an inspiration. "Listen, Josh, call me back at this number at 8:30 p.m. your time. I need to talk to Kathy when she finishes her shift."

Without telling Kathy what was going on, I had her sit in my office while we waited for Josh's call. Right on the money, he called. I put it on speakerphone and started talking. "Josh, Kathy's here with me in the office. I have an idea I hope you both will like. You know I just turned 64. I've had this business for more years than I want to count. I'm tired of getting up at 6:00 a.m. and getting home at 7:00 p.m. Plus, my accountant says I don't need to work; I have plenty of cash in my IRA and 401k, and

49

my Social Security check will be pretty good.

Grandma's house was paid for long ago, as you know.

Katie and her family are pretty well off and don't want

us to sell grandma's house. She says I can live in it for

free.

"So, here's the deal: How about I formally

transfer ownership of the big T-Rx to you two? You

both have a good nose for business, you get along, and

the drivers here know you. What about it?"

Let's just say that if the noise in my office and

coming over the phone line wasn't pandemonium, it

came pretty damn close.

I was out of West Oakland by the end of that

month. Not that I didn't stop by to visit, but my visits

were rare. When I needed something delivered, I

knew who to call.

www.ingramcontent.com/pod-product-compliance
Lightning Source LLC
Chambersburg PA
CBHW071220130626
46555CB00004B/1778